Willy visits the Square World

Jeffrey Archer

Illustrated by Derek Matthews

OCTOPUS

Willy lived in a small house in Cambridge, with his Mum and Dad, his younger brother Jamie, Randolph the bear, and Yo-Yo the cat.

Willy was a happy boy who enjoyed adventures and games. He worked very hard at school and although he never came top of the class everybody liked him. He shared all his secrets and sweets with his friend, Randolph Bear, who was awfully good at sums in his head but not very good at reading.

Randolph had been made for Willy's mother when she was a little girl by Great Aunt Knewstubb. He was a large brown bear with amber eyes and a fat tummy, which came from eating too many of Willy's sweets and not taking enough exercise.

Willy and Randolph were sitting in bed in their room at the top of the stairs, waiting for Mum to read them a story. Mum always seemed to take a long time to clear up after Willy had had a bath, probably because Willy always managed to splash so much water on the floor. While they waited, Randolph told Willy a secret.

'Mum doesn't listen to me any more,' said Randolph sadly, his furry paws placed across his big tummy.

'Why not?' asked Willy, buttoning up his pyjamas which were just a little too big for him.

'I don't know,' said Randolph. 'She stopped when she grew up. Grown-ups never listen to toys.'

'When I grow up, I'll still listen to toys,' said Willy. 'And so will Jamie.'

They both looked over to the next bed where Willy's brother, Jamie, had given up waiting for his bedtime story and was already fast asleep.

Just then, Mum came running up the stairs looking very worried.

'I can't find Yo-Yo anywhere, Willy. Have you seen him? He hasn't been back to the house since teatime. He seems to have disappeared.'

'No, I haven't seen him.' said Willy. 'Why don't you ask Randolph?'

'Don't be cheeky, Willy,' said Mum, 'this is no laughing matter.'

She turned the light out and left the room without even saying goodnight to Willy or Randolph and quite forgot about their bedtime story.

'See what I mean,' said Randolph. 'Doesn't bother to ask me anymore. Not that I know where Yo-Yo is. But I expect he won't be far from a fire or a tin of cat food.'

'You don't think someone has stolen him, do you?' said Willy.

'Oh, I hope not, because he is such a friendly little cat and will talk to anyone,' said Randolph.

From downstairs, they could hear Mum talking to Dad about the missing Yo-Yo, so they kept very quiet and listened.

'I've searched high and low for Yo-Yo and I can't think where in the world he is,' Mum was saying.

'What does Mum mean by that?' whispered Willy. 'Are there other worlds?'

'Oh, yes,' said Randolph very knowingly. 'There's Jupiter and Mars and I think there may be one called Timbuktu. They are a very long, long way away.'

'You can't go by bus then?' asked Willy.

'No, the bus doesn't go that far,' said Randolph sounding as if he knew about these things, although he had only been on a bus once before when Mum was a little girl and that was many years ago. 'To reach other worlds you must fly through space.'

They both sat in silence thinking about space travel and looking worried. Then Willy said, 'Dad gave me a space suit for Christmas and he told me I could go anywhere in it. Wait there, Randolph. I'll see if I can find it.' Willy jumped out of bed to look for his space suit.

'Get back into bed, William,' called Mum from downstairs.

Randolph hid under the sheets while Willy tip-toed to the toy cupboard and started searching among the toys who were trying to get some sleep.

'I'm sorry to wake you,' he said. 'But I need my space suit.'

A rather cross red engine puffed, 'It's under the plasticine, Willy.'

'Thank you, red engine,' said Willy, and took out his space suit and closed the toy cupboard and went back to Randolph, who was still under the sheets.

'We must do what we can to find Yo-Yo,' said Willy, as he put on the space suit and looked at the instructions. 'Randolph, do come out from under the sheets. I need you to read the instructions on the label for me.'

Randolph peeped out and started reading the instructions on the space suit.

'Hand wash 30–40°C,' he said. 'No, that can't be right. Hold on, there's a button on your chest marked "blast-off".'

'That must be it, Randolph,' said Willy, 'but how will *you* get there?'

Randolph sat on the end of the bed thinking about the problem, his fluffy head resting on his paw. He certainly didn't want Willy to go looking for Yo-Yo in another world without him.

'I know what to do,' said Randolph. 'I'll hold on to your hand very tightly and when you press the button, we will both travel to the other world together.'

'That's a good idea, Randolph, let's hope it works.'

Randolph held Willy and Willy pressed the button in the middle of his chest while Randolph closed his eyes and clung on tight.

Zangggggggplop —— twelve moments later, they opened their eyes and
there they were in another world, surrounded by friendly little people. Willy
had never seen anything like them before. They were very small and instead of
feet they had springs and they couldn't stop bouncing up and down on the
spot. They had tiny green faces and big red eyes and round flat noses. All the
time they laughed and smiled. Randolph kept hold of Willy's hand because he
was just a bit frightened, although he was much bigger than any of the little
bouncing people.

'Where are we and who are you?' asked Willy, in what he thought was a
firm voice. The fattest of the laughing people bounced forward and said:

'We are the Fuzzies, and you have landed on the light side of the square
world.'

'The light side?' said Willy, puzzled.

'Yes,' said the Fat Fuzzy. 'There are two sides to the square world, a light side and a dark side and you were lucky enough to land on the light side. Why have you come to the square world?' the Fat Fuzzy demanded.

'I have come to find our cat, Yo-Yo,' said Willy.

'Do you know where he is, Mr Fuzzy?' asked Randolph.

'I am afraid I don't,' replied the Fat Fuzzy politely and he turned to the other Fuzzies who bounced up and down and said, 'No,' all together, and then burst out laughing.

'This is no laughing matter,' said Willy severely.

'We're sorry,' said another Fuzzy. 'But we always laugh on the light side of the square world. I think we had better take you to see the wise and venerable Big Whoosh, who knows everything, and he will tell you what has happened to Yo-Yo.'

So all the Fuzzies made a circle around Willy and Randolph, and escorted
them to the Laughing Tree where the wise and venerable Big Whoosh lived.
The Laughing Tree stood in the middle of the light side of the square world
and when they reached it, Willy noticed that all its branches and leaves were
very still.

The Fat Fuzzy cleared his throat:

'These two have come from the round world to seek advice from the wise
and venerable Big Whoosh.'

Willy and Randolph stared at the Laughing Tree, but they could not see
anything but leaves. Then, suddenly, out of a large hole in the trunk of the
tree came a neat little bird with a note pad and a pencil. It hopped along to the
end of the shortest branch and waited. When there was complete silence the
little bird announced 'Big Whoosh' and out of the same hole came a great owl
covered in yellow feathers with one blue eye that Willy could see while the
other was covered with an eyepatch. He hopped to the end of the longest
branch and stared down at Willy and Randolph. He looked very wise and very
venerable, though Willy wasn't sure what venerable meant. All the branches
on the tree clapped their leaves together, applauding Big Whoosh. He raised a
foot and the applause stopped.

'I am Big Whoosh, the cleverest being in the square world, cleverer than
anybody in the round world. To each person who seeks it I give one piece of
advice and no more. Who comes for advice today?'

There was a short silence. Then Willy found his voice:

'Please, Big Whoosh, Randolph and I would like some advice.'

'You may have one piece of advice each and no more,' said Big Whoosh.

The little bird perched on the end of the branch took notes of everything
that Big Whoosh said but wrote down nothing anyone else said.

'Willy,' whispered Randolph, 'let's ask Big Whoosh for only one piece of
advice, in case we need another piece later.'

'That's very clever, Randolph,' said Willy. 'You ask for your piece of
advice now, and I'll save mine for later.'

'Please, Big Whoosh,' said Randolph, 'where is our little cat Yo-Yo?'

Willy and Randolph and all the Fuzzies held their breath while Big
Whoosh stared down at Randolph. After a long pause and some more
blinking, opened his large beak, and surprised everybody by not answering
but demanding, 'describe him.'

'Oh,' said Willy. 'Yo-Yo is four years old and he is a silver-grey tabby
with a long tail and a white fluffy tummy. He will be very frightened if he
thinks he's lost, so Randolph and I have come to find him. Do you know
where he is, Big Whoosh?'

'Of course I do,' said Big Whoosh, 'I know everything.' He paused,
cleared his throat and stared at Willy. 'Yo-Yo has been stolen by Thieving
Bird, messenger and servant of Grumpfuzz, the wicked monster who lives on
the dark side of the square world, on the unhappy island.'

All the little Fuzzies bowed their heads and although they were still
laughing they looked very frightened.

'How do we get there?' asked Willy.

'No, no,' said Randolph. 'Save your piece of advice, Willy, we may need to
know something much more important later.'

Big Whoosh smiled at Randolph benignly.

'You are indeed a very sensible bear considering you come from the round world.'

The branches on the Laughing Tree clapped their leaves together and applauded Randolph, though not as long or as loudly as they had applauded Big Whoosh.

'Please, Big Whoosh, can I ask you a question that's not a question?' asked Randolph.

'How can a question not be a question?' boomed Big Whoosh.

'Well, I only wanted to know what kind of bird is taking notes of everything you say.'

'Don't be silly, Randolph, everybody knows that's a Secretary Bird.'

'Oh, of course' said Randolph, and all the Fuzzies burst out laughing.

'Now be on your way, goodbye and good luck,' said Big Whoosh. 'Return only when you need your other piece of advice.'

Without another word he disappeared into the large hole in the bark of the Laughing Tree to thunderous applause. He was followed by Secretary Bird clutching on to her note pad.

Willy and Randolph weren't sure what to do next.

'How will we get to the dark side of the square world?' said Randolph.

'We will take you to the edge of the light side,' said the second Fuzzy. 'But we dare not take you to the dark side because it is very dangerous and we can't see where to go.'

So once again all the Fuzzies made a circle round Willy and Randolph and then led them to the edge of the light side of the square world.

When they arrived the first Fuzzy shook hands with Willy and said, sounding rather doubtful, 'If you ever return we will be here to meet you and take you back to the wise and venerable big Whoosh for your second piece of advice.'

Then they all bounced away because they were frightened of being so near the dark side.

Willy and Randolph waved goodbye to the Fuzzies and then crawled on their stomachs to the edge of the light side and stared over on to the dark side.

'It doesn't look very friendly,' said Randolph.

'I know but we must be brave, Randolph. It would be terrible to have come all this way and then to return home without Yo-Yo.'

'Yo-Yo? Yo-Yo who? Yo-Yo what? Yo-Yo where?'

Willy and Randolph looked back on to the light side, and there lying along the edge of the square world was a large green snake.

Randolph threw his arms around Willy and began to cry. Willy didn't cry but he *was* very frightened.

'Please don't cry,' said the green snake. 'I'm not like other snakes. I won't bite you, or squeeze you, or poison you, but nobody talks to me because they all think I will which only means I get so lonely.'

'But snakes where we come from can be very dangerous,' said Willy, 'and my Mum told me to keep away from them.'

'I know, I know, but I'm only a glowsnake and I wouldn't harm anybody. I just sit here on the edge of the light side of the square world, telling people not to fall over on to the dark side.'

'But we have to go on to the dark side,' said Willy, 'because Grumpfuzz, the wicked monster, has captured Yo-Yo, our cat, and Randolph Bear and I must rescue him.'

'Oh, that would be very dangerous,' said Glowsnake, 'Grumpfuzz eats anybody who goes to visit him and everybody knows that little furry cats are his favourite breakfast.'

'Then there is no time to lose,' said Willy.

'But you won't be able to see your hand in front of your face on the dark side,' added Glowsnake, 'so how would you find your way to the unhappy island where Grumpfuzz the wicked monster lives?'

'You can take us,' said Willy firmly.

'Oh, at last, somebody trusts me,' hissed Glowsnake happily, and then he did something that amazed Willy and Randolph. He curled himself round and round until he made a ball and then he switched himself on and began to shine with a strong, green light, from his head to his tail.

'Oh! How did you do that?' cried Willy and Randolph together.

'I don't know how I manage it,' said Glowsnake, 'and no one has ever seen me do it before because they all run away before I get the chance to show them. Now you both follow me on to the dark side. While I am switched on, you will be able to see twenty paces in front of you.'

Glowsnake slithered on to the other side of the square world. Willy put his hands over the edge and pulled himself over on to the dark side. Then he put his hands back over the edge and pulled Randolph over to join him. They were both frightened, but Willy remembered poor little Yo-Yo, so he began to walk bravely into the darkness, lit only by the light coming from Glowsnake.

After they had been going for only a few minutes, Willy stopped.

'Can you hear something above us?' he asked. They all listened very hard. A flapping noise in the sky was coming closer and closer. They looked up and, there above them, they saw a very strange sight, a bird flying upsidedown.

'Good gracious,' said Willy. 'An Upsidedown Bird.'

'Perhaps it's Thieving Bird, messenger and servant of Grumpfuzz, the wicked monster,' said Randolph nervously, trying to hide behind Willy.

'I am not Thieving Bird,' said the Upsidedown Bird indignantly, as he flew round and round, staring suspiciously at Glowsnake. 'I am Upsidedown Bird, who has been banished to the dark side of the square world by the wise and venerable Big Whoosh for laughing at the advice he gave me. I can only return to the light side when I have done a very brave deed. I suppose there aren't any brave deeds I could do for you, are there?' he asked hopefully.

'Poor Upsidedown Bird,' said Willy. 'Perhaps I can help you. Why don't you fly us to the unhappy island home of Grumpfuzz and help me rescue my little cat Yo-Yo? That would be very brave and I would tell the wise and venerable Big Whoosh of your courage.'

'I will, I will,' said Upsidedown Bird joyfully, but he was fearful of coming any closer because of Glowsnake.

'Don't be afraid,' said Willy, 'Glowsnake is our friend and guide.'

'I've never heard of a friendly snake, it's most irregular,' said Upsidedown Bird.

'See what I mean?' said Glowsnake. 'What an awful reputation my relations have given me. I've never heard of an Upsidedown Bird, come to that.'

'You're quite safe,' said Randolph to Upsidedown Bird, 'Glowsnake wouldn't dream of hurting you.'

'Hmm,' said Upsidedown Bird doubtfully, but all the same he flew as close to the ground as he could.

'Can't you land?' asked Willy.

'No,' said Upsidedown Bird. 'I meant to ask the wise and venerable Big Whoosh how to land, but I forgot that I could only have one piece of advice, and I asked the wrong question.'

'What did you ask him?' said Randolph.

'How to catch a wormfuzz without landing,' said Upsidedown Bird. 'The wise and venerable Big Whoosh said I would have to do a back somersault, and I laughed.'

'That wasn't very polite of you,' said Willy. 'But I'll tell you what I'll do. If you help me rescue Yo-Yo, I will ask the wise and venerable Big Whoosh how you can land, because I haven't asked for my piece of advice yet.'

'Oh, thank you Willy, you may be my only hope,' said Upsidedown Bird gratefully. 'Climb up on my tummy and I will fly you to Grumpfuzz's island in the middle of the dark side.'

Willy, Randolph and Glowsnake climbed on to Upsidedown Bird, who rose high into the air. They made a strange sight flying through the darkness with only the light from Glowsnake to guide them. They passed clouds and trees and flew on and on for what seemed like hours to Willy.

Suddenly Glowsnake quivered and his tail shone even more brightly. 'I can see Grumpfuzz,' he said, and they all strained their eyes to look. Yes, there he was in the distance, and Willy wasn't at all frightened, because Grumpfuzz looked like a very small monster. But as Upsidedown Bird flew closer and closer, Grumpfuzz grew bigger and bigger. Randolph became so scared that he closed his eyes and covered them with his paws, and wished he'd stayed at home in Cambridge. Upsidedown Bird was lucky that he could not see Grumpfuzz properly, because he was upsidedown.

'Switch yourself off, Glowsnake,' said Willy, 'so that Grumpfuzz can't see us coming.'

So Glowsnake switched himself off and Upsidedown Bird flew on through the darkness towards the unhappy island and the angry Grumpfuzz.

As they flew nearer Willy could just make out in the gloom that
Grumpfuzz was very large and very ugly. He had four thick legs with three
dirty toes at the end of each foot and the longest tail Willy had ever seen. His
flat nose reached his lower lip and his wide, open mouth showed eight tusk-
like black teeth. Grumpfuzz stood right in the middle of the unhappy island,
surrounded by the Prickly Water. Willy looked down and there between two
of his huge toes crouched Yo-Yo looking very small and very frightened, next
to a pot of boiling water with big white letters which read 'Grumpfuzz's
Breakfast.' On the edge of the pot stirring the water with a large wooden
spoon stood an evil bird with untidy black feathers.

'That must be Thieving Bird,' said Willy, but Randolph wouldn't look.

'What shall I do now?' said Upsidedown Bird.

Willy thought hard. 'Stay just out of reach of Grumpfuzz, and fly round
and round the island as fast as you can,' he commanded.

So Upsidedown Bird flew round and round, getting faster and faster. Willy, Randolph and Glowsnake had to cling on very tightly so as not to fall off. The monster's fiery eyes followed them round and round, faster and faster, but Upsidedown Bird was going so fast that Grumpfuzz soon became dizzy trying to follow him going round and round. He became so dizzy that he started to wobble on his huge toes, and lose his balance until finally he fell off his island and into the Prickly Water with a huge splash.

'Down,' cried Willy. 'Switch on, Glowsnake.'

At once the whole island was ablaze with light. Down went Upsidedown Bird, and scooped up Yo-Yo in his large beak, and flew back high into the air. But by then Grumpfuzz had recovered and he leapt furiously out of the Prickly Water back on to his island. Balancing on his long tail he stretched up into the sky, his huge feet clawing at Upsidedown Bird. One of the dirty toes pulled Willy from the tummy of Upsidedown Bird. As Willy fell, he grabbed hold of Yo-Yo, whom Upsidedown Bird had firmly in his beak. Down, down, down, they were dragged inexorably towards the Prickly Water.

As they fell Grumpfuzz clamped his large black teeth into Willy's space suit and tugged and tugged a little too hard and off came the space suit. Suddenly Willy was free, but he only had his pyjamas on.

'Up quickly,' shouted Willy, 'before Grumpfuzz strikes again. Switch yourself off, Glowsnake.'

All was darkness again, and Upsidedown Bird was so frightened that he flew twice as quickly as he had ever flown before. Still he held Yo-Yo firmly in his beak, and Randolph clung on to Glowsnake, and Willy clung fast to Randolph. Through the air they sped, and once again after them followed the evil Grumpfuzz's waving foot, but he could not find Willy in the darkness.

'After them, evil one,' shrieked Grumpfuzz, and into the air flew Thieving Bird, servant and messenger to the monster.

Willy, Randolph, Glowsnake and Yo-Yo held on to each other for dear life. Upsidedown Bird, weighed down as he was, could not fly nearly as fast as Thieving Bird, so slowly but surely Thieving Bird gained on them.

'Oh, Willy,' said Randolph sadly, 'what shall we do?' thinking the end had come.

'I don't know,' replied Willy.

But then Thieving Bird made a silly mistake. He flew to a great height and decided to attack from above, forgetting that Upsidedown Bird was the wrong way up. When he reached them Glowsnake threw himself around Thieving Bird, while Upsidedown Bird caught him in his talons and pecked him sharply in the neck. Blood flowed everywhere. Then Glowsnake uncurled and released him suddenly and he fell down into the Prickly Water and sank like a stone.

'Hooray,' cried Willy and Randolph together.

'Miaow,' said Yo-Yo.

'You have proved how brave you are, Upsidedown Bird, and we shall tell the wise and venerable Big Whoosh,' said Willy.

'Thank you, thank you,' said Upsidedown Bird, and he piloted Willy, Randolph, Yo-Yo and Glowsnake back towards the edge of the light side.

They had to jump off because Upsidedown Bird couldn't land. They were all overjoyed to be back, especially Yo-Yo, although he could only say 'Miaow'.

Waiting for them were all the Fuzzies, bouncing up and down on their springs, laughing happily.

'Welcome back to the light side,' said the Fat Fuzzy.

'Welcome back to the light side,' they all cried as they cheered Willy. 'Where is Randolph?'

Randolph crept over the edge very slowly because he was very fat so they all cheered again. Yo-Yo followed Randolph and they cheered even louder. Then rather shyly Glowsnake slithered over the edge and the cheering stopped and all the Fuzzies started bouncing away.

'Don't bounce away, come back,' said Willy. 'Glowsnake is our friend.'

The Fuzzies watched fearfully at a distance as Willy stroked Glowsnake. They could scarcely believe their eyes and bounced forward to have a closer look.

'It's all right,' said Willy. 'Glowsnake is not like other snakes. You should never judge anyone by their looks.'

He remembered Dad had said that once.

'Switch yourself on for our friends, Glowsnake,' said Willy.

Glowsnake curled up and shone with pride while the Fuzzies bounced around him in silent admiration.

'Very clever, Glowsnake,' Willy said. 'Now I must return to the wise and venerable Big Whoosh for my piece of advice.'

'Yes,' said Randolph. 'We must ask him how to get back to the round world, now that Grumpfuzz, the wicked monster, has gobbled up your space suit and all you have left is your pyjamas.'

'I can't ask that,' said Willy. 'I promised Upsidedown Bird I would find out how he could land.'

'But, Willy, will we ever get back home,' said Randolph. 'If we can't ask the wise and venerable Big Whoosh?'

'I know,' said Willy, 'but I can't break my promise to Upsidedown Bird.'

So they all started walking towards the middle of the light side until they saw afar off the Laughing Tree swaying in the breeze. When it caught sight of Willy, Randolph, Upsidedown Bird, Yo-Yo and Glowsnake, not to mention all the Fuzzies, it became very still and waited for them all to reach the tree. Then out of the large hole in the trunk came Secretary Bird with her note pad and pencil. They all waited in silence. A few seconds later appeared the wise and venerable Big Whoosh, and once again as he marched to the end of the longest branch, and the branches clapped their leaves together, until Big Whoosh raised his foot and the applause stopped.

'I am Big Whoosh. The cleverest person in the square world and cleverer than anyone in the round world. Who comes for advice today?'

'I do,' said Willy. 'But first I have come to tell you that Upsidedown Bird was very brave and helped me to rescue my cat Yo-Yo from Grumpfuzz, the wicked monster.'

'Umm ...' said Big Whoosh portentously. 'That pleases me and as a reward I will release him for ever from the dark side of the square world.'

The branches of the Laughing Tree clapped their leaves together politely to applaud Upsidedown Bird, who flapped his wings in triumph.

'What advice do you seek, Willy?' enquired Big Whoosh, who considered that Upsidedown Bird had had quite enough applause.

'How can Upsidedown Bird land?' asked Willy.

'Are you sure that is what you want to know?'

'Yes,' said Willy.

'I would rather know how to get back home,' said Randolph in a quiet voice.

'Silence, Randolph,' said Big Whoosh, 'you have had your piece of advice, and you may not ask again. Willy, are you certain that you are asking the right question? Think carefully before you reply.'

'Yes I'm certain,' said Willy. 'I made a promise and now I must keep it.'

'So be it,' said Big Whoosh. 'I will pronounce.'

They all fell silent.

'The only way that Upsidedown Bird can ever land is to fly to the round world, because there everybody is upsidedown, though they don't know it because no one has ever told them, but at least there Upsidedown Bird will appear to be a Rightwayup Bird.'

'Oh, thank you, thank you, wise and venerable Big Whoosh,' said
Upsidedown Bird, 'and thank you, Willy.'

The branches clapped their leaves in admiration for the wise and venerable
Big Whoosh, who once again disappeared into the trunk of the Laughing Tree
before the applause had died down. The Secretary Bird tiptoed in after him.

'Come on, Willy, come on, Randolph, come on, Yo-Yo, I can take you
home,' cried Upsidedown Bird joyfully.

Willy, Randolph and Yo-Yo climbed on to Upsidedown Bird and waved
goodbye to Glowsnake who was switching himself on and off while playing
happily with his new friends the Fuzzies. Away they flew back to the round
world, a journey which took twelve moments.

In the morning, Mum came up to draw the curtains. There perched on a
tree in the garden was Rightwayup Bird so obviously guarding Yo-Yo from
any future attempts at catnapping. Mum turned to wake up Willy and when
she saw Yo-Yo asleep at the end of the bed, she rushed back down the stairs
calling to Dad.

'I've found Yo-Yo – he was asleep at the end of Willy's bed all the time.'

'But Mum,' said Willy only half awake now, sitting up in bed, 'that's just
not true. Randolph and I . . .'

'Shhh,' said Randolph. Willy stared at the fat brown bear, who was fully
awake.

'Why shouldn't we tell Mum what really happened?' said Willy.

'Because grown-ups never listen,' said Randolph.

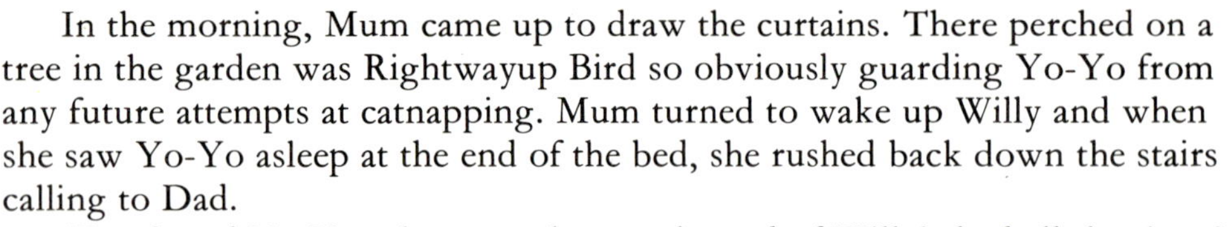